A Fire Engine for Ruthie

by Lesléa Newman

Illustrated by Cyd Moore

Clarion Books/New York

Clarion Books
a Houghton Mifflin Company imprint
215 Park Avenue South, New York, NY 10003
Text copyright © 2004 by Lesléa Newman
Illustrations copyright © 2004 by Cyd Moore

The illustrations were rendered in watercolor.
The text was set in 24-point Aunt Mildred.

www.houghtonmifflinbooks.com

Printed in Singapore

Library of Congress Cataloging-in-Publication Data

Newman, Lesléa.
A fire engine for Ruthie / by Lesléa Newman ; illustrated by Cyd Moore.
p. cm.
Summary: Ruthie's Nana suggests playing tea party and fashion show during their visit, but Ruthie is
much more interested in the vehicles that a neighbor boy is playing with as they pass his house each day.
ISBN 0-618-15989-4
[1. Play—Fiction. 2. Trucks—Fiction. 3. Toys—Fiction. 4. Grandmothers—Fiction.] I. Moore, Cyd, ill. II. Title.
PZ7.N47988Fi 2004
[E]—dc22   2003022791

ISBN-13: 978-0-618-15989-5
ISBN-10: 0-618-15989-4

TWP 10 9 8 7 6 5 4 3 2 1

for Susanna Stein
Vroom! Vroom! Vroom!

—L. N.

in memory of my mother

—C. M.

n the first day of Ruthie's visit to her
grandmother's house, Ruthie and Nana walk to
the grocery store to buy Ruthie's favorite foods.

On their way home, they pass Brian's house. Ruthie shields her eyes from the sun to watch Brian playing in his front yard with a fire engine. A red fire engine with a black-and-white dog sitting up front and a silver ladder that slides up and down and a yellow hose to unwind and a siren that goes **whee-ooh! whee-ooh! whee-ooh!**

"Do you have a fire engine to play with at your house, Nana?" Ruthie asks.

"No," says Nana, "but I have some beautiful dolls waiting at home for you."

Nana opens an old trunk, takes out her dolls, and sits them all around the kitchen table. "Why don't we have a tea party?" she asks Ruthie.

"Okay," Ruthie says, even though she doesn't really like tea parties.

Ruthie pretends to pour some tea for Nana. Then she twitches her nose in the air. "Do you smell smoke?" she asks Nana. "Fire! Fire!"

Ruthie puts all the dolls into a cardboard box and pretends they're racing across town to put out a fire. But the cardboard box has no black-and-white dog sitting up front. The cardboard box has no silver ladder that slides up and down and no yellow hose to unwind. The cardboard box doesn't make any noise at all.

On the second day of Ruthie's visit, Ruthie and Nana walk to the library to check out Ruthie's favorite books. On their way home, they pass Brian's house again. Ruthie holds her umbrella with one hand and waves to Brian, who is playing on his front porch with a train. A blue train that has two cars and a little red caboose and wheels that go **chucka-chucka, chucka-chucka** and a whistle that goes **toot! toot!**

"Do you have a train to play with at your house, Nana?" Ruthie asks.

"No," says Nana, "but I have some lovely dress-up clothes waiting at home for you."

Nana takes a bag of dress-up clothes out of the closet, spills them onto the living room couch, and puts on a floppy orange hat and white shoes with high heels and silver clasps. "Why don't we have a fashion show?" she asks Ruthie.

"Okay," Ruthie says, even though she doesn't really like fashion shows.

Ruthie puts on a pink flowered skirt and purple gloves with pearl buttons. Then she cups her hand around her ear. "Do you hear a train?" she asks Nana.

Ruthie pulls a fuzzy blue beret over her ears and pretends it's an engineer's cap. "All aboard!" she shouts. "Tickets, please." Ruthie pushes some chairs together to make a train. But the chairs don't have wheels that go **chucka-chucka, chucka-chucka** or a whistle that goes **toot! toot!**

On the third day of Ruthie's visit, Ruthie and Nana walk to the playground to swing on Ruthie's favorite swing set. On their way home, they pass Brian's house once more. Ruthie holds her hat so the wind won't blow it away and calls out "Hi!" to Brian, who is playing in his driveway with a motorcycle. A red motorcycle with shiny handlebars that turn left and right and a bright, white headlight that really works and two brown saddlebags to put things in and a button to press that goes **vroom! vroom! vroom!**

"Do you have a motorcycle to play with at your house, Nana?" Ruthie asks.

"No," says Nana, "but I have some pretty paints waiting at home for you."

Nana takes some jars of paint out of the cabinet, opens them up, and gives Ruthie a piece of paper and a paintbrush. "Why don't we paint some flowers?" she asks Ruthie.

"Okay," Ruthie says, even though she doesn't really like painting flowers. Ruthie paints a yellow daisy and then looks out the window. "Do you see a motorcycle?" she asks Nana. Ruthie paints a motorcycle right next to her flower.

When Ruthie is done with her painting, Nana gives her a new piece of paper, and Ruthie paints another motorcycle. She paints big motorcycles and little motorcycles. They all have shiny handlebars and bright, white headlights and brown saddlebags to put things in, but they don't have any buttons to press that go **vroom! vroom! vroom!** Ruthie paints lots of pictures, and Nana hangs them up to dry all over the house.

On the fourth day of Ruthie's visit, Nana looks at all of Ruthie's pictures and then she looks at Ruthie. "What would you like to do today?" she asks.

Ruthie thinks hard. She thinks about Brian playing with his fire engine. She thinks about Brian playing with his train. She thinks about Brian playing with his motorcycle. Ruthie tells Nana, "I want to play with Brian."

When Ruthie arrives at Brian's house, Brian is in his room playing with his toys. Brian takes out the shiny red fire engine. "Look, Ruthie," he says. "This is where the fire chief sits."

Ruthie takes out the long blue train. "Look, Brian," she says. "This is where the engineer sits."

Brian takes out the big red motorcycle. "Look, Ruthie," he says. "This is where the driver sits."

Brian and Ruthie take out cars and trucks and buses, and play with them all.

When Nana comes to take Ruthie home, Ruthie is so busy playing that she doesn't see Nana standing in the doorway. When Nana says, "Ruthie, it's time to put everything away," Ruthie is so busy playing that she doesn't even hear her. Nana starts putting away Brian's toys. She picks up the blue train and heads for Brian's toy box.

"Stop the train! Stop the train!" Ruthie calls. "I need to go to my nana's house."

Nana looks at the toy in her hand. She kneels down and races the train over to Ruthie. **"Chucka-chucka, chucka-chucka, toot! toot!"** Nana looks at Ruthie. "Do you have your ticket?" she asks.

"Yes, I do," says Ruthie. "Does this train stop at my nana's house?"

"It certainly does," says Nana. "All aboard!"

"Taxi! Taxi!" Brian calls.

Nana looks around and sees a yellow taxi. **"Beep! Beep! Beep!"** She races the car over to Brian. "Did you call a taxi?" she asks.

"Yes, I did," says Brian. "I need to go to Market Street right away."

"Hop in," says Nana.

Ruthie and Nana and Brian play with tow trucks, moving vans, and cement mixers. They play with dump trucks, school buses, and tractor-trailers. When Brian's mother comes upstairs, Ruthie and Nana and Brian are so busy playing that they don't see her standing in the doorway. When Brian's mother says, "It's time to put everything away," Ruthie and Nana and Brian are so busy playing that they don't even hear her.

On the last day of Ruthie's visit, Ruthie and Nana walk to the toy shop to buy their favorite toys. Nana buys a fire engine for Ruthie, a train for herself, and two motorcycles to share.

Whee-ooh! Whee-ooh! Whee-ooh!
Chucka-chucka, chucka-chucka, toot! toot!
Vroom! Vroom! Vroom!